# The Misadventure of a Christmas Elf

*or*
*How Christmas magic was lost and found*

## By Nancy Potts
## Illustrations by Daniel Kinney

This book is dedicated to *Maureen*.
Without her I would have never met Santa's elf, Elmer.

Published in 2020 by Westie Publishing
Enon, OH 45323

First Edition

Potts, Nancy
*The Misadventure of a Christmas Elf*
Story by Nancy Potts
Illustrations by Daniel Kinney

ISBN 978-1-7340061-7-9 (paperback)

**E**lmer the Elf looked up at the sparkling stars in the black velvet sky and sighed. "Only two days until Christmas," he told himself. "It's time to return home to Christmas Village." He slipped his hand into his pants pocket to retrieve his magic crystal. Something was wrong. He couldn't feel it anywhere. "Maybe I put it in another pocket." He searched his other pants pocket and the pockets in his jacket. No crystal. He rechecked the first pocket. "Oh, no, there's a hole in my pocket. It must have fallen out but where and when?" He put his tiny hands on his cherry red cheeks and groaned. "This is terrible, just terrible. What am I going to do? How am I going to get home? On my! Oh dear! Such a fix! If I don't get home, Santa won't know who to bring presents to!" Elmer stuffed his hands into his jacket pockets and wandered up and down snowy Evergreen Street.

He stopped in front of a small red brick house and shivered. It was getting colder and he needed to find a warm place to spend the night. He wandered to the back of the house and peeked in the kitchen window. The house was dark and quiet. Everyone was asleep. He could pop inside for the night and be gone before anyone was up in the morning. There was only one problem. Without the crystal his magic only worked backwards and there were certain things he couldn't do.

"Well, here goes nothing." Elmer thought about going outside, tugged three times on his right earlobe and said the magic words *LEGNA SAMTSIRHC*.

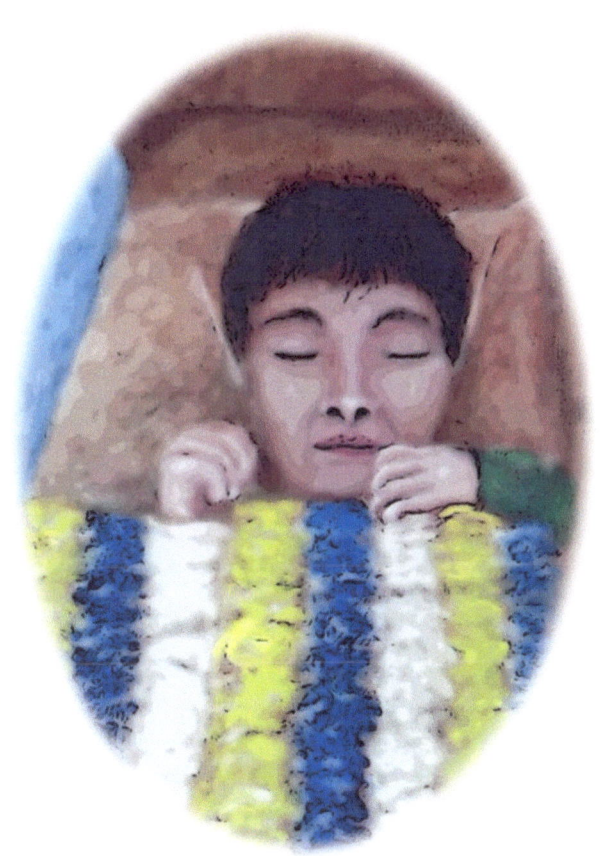

He looked around and did a little dance. "Hooray! It worked!" He congratulated himself, hopped up on the living room sofa, wiggled under the warm afghan and fell asleep.

During the night he dreamed of all the children he had checked on for Santa this year. There was Jenny frosting doughnuts at her father's bakery. Kendra reading to her little brother, Bryan at the pond tying Liz's and Julie's ice skates, and Matt running to the grocery store for his grandmother. Then there was Abby.

All at once he was dreaming that it was raining and he was surrounded by rotting fish. "Phew!" he mumbled and opened one eye. A huge wet pink tongue licked his face. Elmer nearly jumped out of his socks. A pair of large brown eyes stared at him while a cold wet nose sniffed his red knit hat. "Nice doggie. Now shoo, away with you." Elmer burrowed deeper under the afghan to get out of the dog's reach. The dog began to bark. "Sh! Be quiet, you silly animal. You'll wake everyone up!"

"Hugo!" a little girl called, running into the living room. Elmer jumped off the sofa and dived behind the draperies with the dog snapping at his boot heels. "What are you barking at, boy?" The little girl slowly pulled back the curtain and stared at the elf. "Wh … who are you?" she asked.

Elmer blinked his bright blue eyes and smiled nervously. "Would you believe I'm a new kid that just moved into the neighborhood?"

"Nooo," the little girl said as she kneeled down beside him.

"How about, I'm a figment of your imagination?"

"Na huh," she answered, shaking her blond ponytail.

"Well, I can see you're too smart for me, Abby O'Brian. The truth is I'm Elmer, one of Santa Claus' elves. It's my job to check up on all the children for him."

Abby's eyes widened with wonder. "Really and truly?"

"Yes, really and truly," said the elf. Abby threw her arms around him and hugged him tight. "Hey! Take it easy."

She released him and sat back on her heels. "Sorry. So, is that why you're at my house?"

"Not exactly," Elmer said. "I'm here because I can't get back home."

"Why?"

"That's a long story," he said and sat down on the floor next to her. He told her about losing his crystal and how Santa was counting on him to bring the list of good boys and girls before Christmas Eve. "So, you see, I'm really in a pickle."

Abby tucked her nightgown around her legs and stared thoughtfully at her pink bunny slippers. "So, what will happen if you don't get back in time? Will Santa deliver presents to everyone even if he doesn't know who's been good or not?"

Slowly Elmer shook his head. "I'm afraid that's not the way it works. If Santa doesn't have the list, no one will get any presents."

"That doesn't seem fair. What about all the letters kids sent him?"

Elmer shrugged his shoulders. "It won't make any difference. He won't deliver presents without my report." He looked out the window and saw the sun coming up. "Well, I've got to get going. I have a lot of ground to cover and not much time left."

"If I knew what your crystal looked like, maybe I could help find it," Abby told him.

"I suppose you could look around your house and maybe at some of your friends' houses if your mother will let you visit them. My crystal looks like a tiny heart with little smooth flat sides carved all around and it will fit in the palm of your hand. If you hold it in the sunshine, you can see all the colors of the rainbow. Of course, you can't tell anyone what you're doing. It has to be a secret." Elmer pulled his hat down tighter on his head and put on his mittens. "After all, you are the first human to see me in 130  years. Most people don't even know I exist." He gave her a wink, tugged on his earlobe three times, said the magic words, *LEGNA SAMTSIRHC*, and disappeared.

All day Elmer retraced his steps from the day before. He searched the library, the school, the playground, the ice-covered pond, the bakery and all the shops on Main Street. He even sifted through the garbage bins. Ugh! There wasn't even a sniff of his crystal.

In the park he stopped near the ancient ginkgo tree to watch the children sledding. He saw little Jason Jordon pulling his little sister on his sled. "Well, that's a change," Elmer muttered. "Now I can erase that black mark next to his name. I knew he was really a good kid at heart."

The sky was getting darker and the street lights were coming on. Slowly Elmer trudged back toward Abby's house. "That crystal has to be in this town, it just has to be. I hope little Abby has had better luck." When he reached her house, he hopped up on the windowsill outside her bedroom. Her room was empty.

"As long as I'm here, I might as well go inside where it's warm," he decided. He tugged on his earlobe and repeated the magic words.

While he waited for Abby to finish supper, he looked around her room. He could have dropped his crystal here just as easily as anywhere else. He searched her toy chest, her dresser, her closet and under her bed. It wasn't anywhere. He sat down among the stuffed animals at the foot of her bed and scratched his chin. "I've let Santa down. If I ever make it back home, he's going to reassign me to stable duty. I'll never get to come South again to see the children."

Elmer sniffed and wiped his nose with his coat sleeve. In the hallway, he heard Abby and her mother so he jumped under the bed.

"Put on your nightgown and brush your teeth, Abby. I'll be back in a few minutes to tuck you in," her mother said. Abby ran to her window and anxiously looked outside before going into the bathroom to get ready for bed.

When she returned Elmer watched her open her dresser drawer and remove a little wooden treasure box she kept there. She quickly took something from the box. As she put the object in her nightgown pocket, it began to glow bright green and hum. It was his magic crystal! Yes! She had found it! He was so happy he jumped up and hit his head on her bed springs.

"Ow!" he yelped and rubbed the bump forming on the top of his head.

Abby peeked under the bed's dust ruffle. "Oh, it's you," she said and frowned.

"Of course it's me," Elmer whispered. "What's wrong? You don't look very happy to see me."

She quietly closed her bedroom door and he hopped up onto her bed. "I'm happy to see you. I just wasn't expecting you, that's all."

"Well, I'm happy to see you, too. I'm even happier to see that you found my crystal."

"What do you mean?" Abby asked suspiciously. "I don't have your crystal."

Elmer crinkled his brow. "Yes you do. It glowed and sang when you put it in your nightgown pocket. It knows I'm here."

Abby looked in her pocket. "This is a piece of glass. I found it in the backyard this afternoon."

"Look again," Elmer told her. A bright green light filled the pocket.

"I can't hear it sing," Abby insisted. "Are you positive you can't go home without it?"

Elmer stared at her. "Only elves can hear its music and, yes, I definitely need it to return home. What is the matter, Abby? This morning you were excited to help me find it."

"I know, but that was before I found it and saw how pretty it is. I've never seen anything so beautiful. I was hoping I could keep it and … and I could give it to my mother for Christmas."

"Oh, Abby, Abby, there's nothing I'd like better than to let you give such a wonderful present to your mother. The problem is it isn't mine to give, it belongs to Santa. Even if I could give it to you, it isn't the gift your mother wants from you."

"How do you know?"

"Because I'm an elf. If you can keep a secret, I'll show you how I know. Can you?" Abby quickly nodded her head yes. "Okay, take the crystal from your pocket and put it in my hand. Now, put your hands around mine. Can you feel that?"

"Oh, yes," Abby whispered. It made her feel all warm and happy.

"Now, close your eyes and think about your mother. Can you hear her talking to you?"

"Yes."

"What is she saying?"

"The best presents come from the heart, when we do something nice for someone."

Elmer stood on his tiptoes and kissed her forehead. "That's right. It's the most special gift you can give."

Abby smiled at him and took her hands away. "I think I knew that all along. Thank you," she said and gave him a gentle hug.

"You're welcome. Now, I must be going. There's only one more day until Christmas and there's still lots and lots to do." He jumped up on the windowsill and held the crystal heart in both hands. Now that all his magic was back he didn't need to repeat magic words backwards anymore. He smiled at Abby and gave her a wink.

He thought about Christmas Village, tugged on his left earlobe, whispered to the crystal and disappeared! In the silence, the magic words echoed in Abby's ears, **CHRISTMAS ANGEL!**

### Nancy Potts

Nancy Potts is a former staff writer, columnist, and editorial editor for the *Fairborn Daily Herald*. She was also a staff writer for the *Beavercreek Daily News* and a freelance writer for the *Dayton Daily News*. As a journalist, she covered everything from human-interest stories, to murder trials.

After leaving the newspaper business, she went to work for the National Aviation Hall of Fame (NAHF) as their communications coordinator. At the NAHF she wrote for their quarterly magazine and designed several pages for children in the publication. She also researched and wrote video scripts on the inductees for enshrinement. Additionally Nancy wrote many of the enshrinee biographies for their educational display and website.

As an Air Force wife, Nancy has had numerous opportunities to volunteer both in the United States and overseas. She has taught art to kindergarteners in England and tutored grade-schoolers in the States. Nancy has also shared her love of scouting with girls from the east coast to the Arizona desert to Fairborn, Ohio. She has served as a leader, neighborhood chairperson and as public relations chairperson.

Nancy graduated with a degree in Mass Communications from Wright State University. She has been a member of the Society of Children's Book Writers and Illustrators for over 20 years and enjoys writing books for children and teens.

She lives in Enon, Ohio, with her husband Bob and their two adorable dogs, Bonnie and Leo.

### Daniel R. Kinney

Daniel R. Kinney is a talented self-taught artist. He has loved art since he was young and it has always been a side passion for him. After retiring from American Electric Power, he has had more time to focus on his love of painting. Dan lives with his wife, Diana, in Columbus, Ohio. He has been a friend of the author and her husband since high school.